INDIAN ZAIKA

SPECTRUM OF THOUGHTS
A UNIT OF FANATIXX

Indian Zaika

SPECTRUM OF THOUGHTS
A unit of FanatiXx

AM/56, Basanti Colony, Rourkela 769012, Odisha

Website: www.fanatixx.in

"INDIAN ZAIKA"

ISBN: 978-93-89106-42-8

Anthology of English and Hindi Poems & Write-ups 1st Edition

Book Formatting: Saizal Gupta

Cover Design: Ashutosh Das

Disclaimer

2

This book is a collection of poems and articles. Our editors have made their efforts to edit the work of our co-authors, all the poems, quotes have been placed unique in this book.

We have tried our best to check for plagiarism in the write-ups featured in the book, the book consists only the original write-ups.

Acknowledgement

The completion of this book would not have been possible without the hard work of all the co-writers and the core members of FanatiXx Publications. A huge thanks to the core team who have given a hundred percent to this book.

We would also like to thank each one of you who believed in us and brought this book.

A big thanks to all the writers for their immense support and patience.

Above all, thanks to God and parents for blessings and love.

Contents

भारत का निर्माण कुछ इस प्रकार 6

Compiler's Biography 8

दिल्ली 10

मध्य प्रदेश 13

Indore-Heart of M.P 17

My Nagaland 21

Shivamogga 24

Andhra Pradesh.. 27

Uttrakhand- The Land of Gods 31

Welcome to Thiruvananthapuram 34

Gujarat 36

Andhra Pradesh and Food 39

My Village is My World 43

Hindu Fest 47

Meghalya 51

The Mirchi City 56

A Sweet & Sour Trip to the Kitchen of Traditional Bengali Cuisine 59

A note from the Author 64

" सारे जहाँ से अच्छा हिन्दोस्ताँ हमारा।"

– *Muhammad Iqbal*

भारत का निर्माण कुछ इस प्रकार

-Smriti Ashra

आशाओं के बीज को
आज फिर से बोएंगे हम ,
ये झंडा लहराएंगे
और शान से कहेंगे हम ,
आज़ाद हिन्द के ये
आज़ाद पंछी है हम ।

दानवों का नाश करना ही
देवताओं का धर्म है ,
वैसे ही कुछ सत्य सा
फौजी का भी कर्म है ।

बीज बोया है साहस का
पसीना भी खून बन जाएगा ,
मेरे देश का वो फ़ौजी है
जो मौत से भी लड़ जाएगा ।

जिससे कहते है हम तिरंगा
वो अनेक रंगों का प्रतीक है ,
अनेकता में एकता ही
हम भारतीयों की सीख है ।

Indian Zaika

भारत हमारा महान है
जिसका करते हम गुणगान है ,
इस देश के हम गर्वीय नागरिक
भारत मां को करते सलाम है ,
देश आबाद रहे हमारा
यही दुआ करते है हम ।

आशाओं के बीज को
आज फिर से बोएंगे हम ,
ये झंडा लहराएंगे
और शान से कहेंगे हम ,
आज़ाद हिन्द के ये
आज़ाद पंछी है हम ।

Compiler's Biography
Smriti Ashra

Smriti Ashra is a very ambitious and passionate writer. She is from literature background. She is blessed with parents who work as a support system and is her backbone at every step. Walls of her body are made up of love, respect. She has been a competent writer in the Anthologies named *'Memories I can't forget'*, *'Pretty little words'*, *'It's Contagious'*, *'1000 Women'*, *'Contrivances of sentiments'*, etc. She has also contributed her write ups in her college E-magazine named *'Qalam'* during her 3 successive years of graduation. She has compiled a dream book named 'Dream-O-Dream'. She loves to dance and act. She is an open book, anyone can read it, but a few ones can make it till the end. She is a bundle of joy and emits the rays of hope and peace.

दिल्ली

-Megha Gupta

कहने को दिलों का ताज है दिल्ली ,
बादशाह की हुकूमत का राज है दिल्ली ।

किस्से, कहानी, हर दिल में कुछ अलग से हैं,
रंग इस शहर के जैसे शराब से हैं,
जो आता है दिल्ली का होजाता है,
इन गलियों में हर कोई खो जाता है ।

यहां सवेरा जैसे चंचलता का प्रतीक हो,
दोपहर में एक रिक्शा भी ना नसीब हो,
शामें , अपना अलग ही राग गुनगुनाती हैं,
और दिल्ली की रातें,
रातें जैसे इशक करना सिखाती हैं।

दिल्ली के धुएं में,
कभी कभी धुंधला जाता है दिल,
सब कुछ है इस शहर में,
फिर भी कभी ना जाने क्यों मिलती नहीं मंज़िल,
सफर के राही सिफर में सिमट जाते हैं,
कुछ लोग जो सवेरे निकलते हैं
शाम को लौटकर नहीं आते हैं।

मेरी ये दिल्ली , दिलवालों की ज़रूर है
पर सभी दिलवालों के पास दिल है क्या?
ऐसे सवाल मेरे मन में रोज़ आते हैं।।

<u>Megha Gupta</u>

Megha is 21 years old, Delhite. Currently working as an illustrator for a children's book, she has worked in many other anthologies. She has worked with media houses like Terribly Tiny Tales and looks forward to reach new heights in the field. Her course of study involves association with the education system of the country and she wants to bring about a change in the system. She is usually passionate about life and says that whatever she is today, the credit goes to her mother.

मध्य प्रदेश

-Anshi Shrivastava

सुनो सुनो एक आवाज़ आई है।
सुनो सुनो मेरे गांव से पैग़ाम लाई है।।

सुनो सुनो मेरी धड़कनें भी कह रही।
कि मेरे दिल में खुशी की लहर छाई है।।

सुनो सुनो वो हवाओं का सरसराना।
सुनो सुनो वो पानी का छलछलाना।।

सुनो सुनो उन बादलों ने भी कहा।
कि खेतों में नई बौर आई है।।

सुनो सुनो वो भीमबेटका की कहानियां।
सुनो सुनो वो महाकाल की बढाईयां।।

सुनो सुनो सांची ने ये दर्शाया है। (सांची स्तूप)
कि अशोका ने भी शांति को अपनाया है।।

सुनो सुनो वो वीर गाथाऐं।
सुनो सुनो वो नवाबों की व्यथाऐं।।

सुनो सुनो इतिहास भी ये दोहराता है। (झांसी की रानी)
कि औरत का मान सबसे ऊपर आता है।।

सुनो सुनो वो पचमढ़ी का कोलाहल।
सुनो सुनो वो पांडवों का पुराना घर।। (पांडव गुफा)

सुनो सुनो वो मां की खुशी।
कि बेटों ने मंदिर बनाया है।। (भोजपुर का मंदिर)

सुनो सुनो वो पेड़ों की झनकार।
सुनो सुनो वो शेर की दहाड़।। (कान्हा नेशनल पार्क)

सुनो सुनो मोरों ने भी पर फैलाए हैं।
कि मेरे मध्यप्रदेश को देखने महमान आए हैं।।

(अतिथि देवो भव:)

<u>Anshi Shrivastava</u>

Anshi Shrivastava, a graduate of B.Com Honours from Bhopal School of Social Sciences in Bhopal city of Madhya Pradesh (India). She admits to being emotional but a practical girl. While her sensitive and conservative temperament has made her somewhat of an introvert, it motivates her to write. Her poems reflect her feelings and are a means of self-expression. In addition to writing, she loves to explore the field of art with her raw skills of sketching, painting and singing. She is fond of writing poems and also quotes. She takes writing as a means to escape reality and explore her imaginary world. More than reality she nourishes her dream world. The imaginary world of her own helps her to see the reality world in a positive way. This helps her to positively react to every situation which also helps her to maintain her kindness and control her temper in every situation. This makes her somewhat childish but she still stays happy with her childish behaviour as she thinks it's better to be kind as child than to be cruel as an adult. She is also fond of animals other than art stuff.

Indore-Heart of M.P

-Ashutosh Das

"Train no. 11056 coming from Kolkata to Indore via. Patna, Lucknow, Bhopal arrives on platform no. 4…..Indore junction welcomes the passengers and wishes for a pleasant stay, thank you ! "So she is finally here after all!" A best friend found online, no less than a family" . I took a deep breath and smiled listening to the announcements. I waved hands while the train was still moving and she was standing on one door! As the train stopped she jumped out of it, the next moment she was hugging me Tight! This was the first time we were meeting, we have known each other for 2 Years for now, I said to her "Welcome to Indore Riya, I am glad that we met "Hahaha! Yes Jay! Am finally here in Indore meeting you.

So now I am going to do all that you told me about it the last time we discussed Indore!" Her eyes were full of stars " Yes of course, but first let's go home and you have some rest" holding like I was trying to hold the jumping frog While at Way back home, I remembered the talk where I described my Indore to her the first time! "So tell me about your city what is it about?" she asked with having no intention to drop it " So my City Indore the heart of M.P. The most simple way to describe it is '*The cleanest city in India*'. Well, no wonder why its 3time No.1 in it after being here!" And laughed like a baby before continuing further " Indore is Foody placed, Everyone here is in love with the food and especially Street food and you know what!

There is a place called *Chappan (56) *! And if you are wondering why 56! Well, there are 56 stores in line and they mostly are of foods and it was M.P first certified Hygiene place of street food! Dam so many awesome moments I have, I just can't wait to create one with you! Talk about food Indore's famous morning snack is *Poha-jalebi* am, telling you this I got water in my mouth" making noises of tasty food feelings.

"Telling you on that Its not just the day we all here are crazy about food! Well, even for midnight we good place called Saraffa which opens at 10 pm and runs to 4 am and it's all about just food, of a crazy night out perfect hanging out spot" I stopped to take the breath. "Damn You endure you all just food food food! Don't have any work or what!" And she started laughing! " No, no! Well, one of the major attraction of the city is the Ganesha ji Temple *Khajrana mandir*.

It's so beautiful dam you can't miss the beauty of its at night! Talking about that. We also got some amazing waterfalls in a radius of 10 km around us and it's worth going! The point to be noted is.

From the waterfall, you have to come in the rainy season! We also Got Rajwada a prime location of buying items like dresses, utensils, books, jewelry, etc! You will never think of going there during the wedding season, its a mess dam mess! Well, that's basic Indore for you with flavors of food, peoples and trends. Visit once and you will say its a mini Mumbai!" I proudly announced as if my Indore is a different country "Dam…. I just can't imagine being there, I promise we will meet in Indore only very soon! Like Very soon!" She said And I heard her voice saying again, but this time she was out of the car.

"Let's go fast I want to see the Indore now!" And she rushed inside the house hugging my mom as if they knew them all before that's reason never introduce your girl best friend to your mom, well just because you get out the cast in your own house!

Knock knock where are you going? Yes, you! How's the Indore? Well, Stay a while and you will know it! I am waiting to see you! Now bye bye

<u>Ashutosh Das</u>

Ashutosh Das, born on 10th Oct '98 is born and brought up in Bihar and currently settled in Indore. He Is pursuing a Degree in B. Visual Arts. For hi writing is eternal . One can contact him through his Instagram handle I.e. @mr.ash

My Nagaland

-*Neirietunuo Miasalhou*

Nagaland the land of festivals,
Surrounded by breathtaking Valleys,
Inhabited by tribal groups,
Kohima the core of the state,
Mithun the state animal,
Blythe's tragopan as state bird,
Rhododendron as state flower, Alder as state tree,
It's rich diversity is obscured,
It's cuisine of food is unique,
It's vibrant folk musics and folk dances inherited.
Each tribe with its own dialect,
Colourful attires with limitless beauty.
Nagaland is conspicuous and not inconspicuous,
It is exoteric and not esoteric,
Introspect is what you must do.
Nagaland is of numerous tribes,
Mountainous ranges is what people throng to see,
Head hunting in Nagaland is now obsolete,
Out of many festivals the widely known "Hornbill festival"
making my Land known to the world.

Indian Zaika

My homeland is known for its hospitality,
It's a dreamland to many,
No camera can do just and no season lessen it's beauty,
Pleasing weather that Pleases each.
I bet you'll wish to stay in my homeland once you
introspect.
Nagaland is a gateway to paradise,
Come and experience the Mother Nature.

<u>Neirietunuo Miasalhou</u>

Neirietounuo miasalhou, is pursuing her BA COURSE AT BAPTIST COLLEGE KOHIMA. she aspire to become an administrator yet she has the passion in writing. She is a gourmet, love playing outdoor games, love reading novels etc. 'Put trust in God and have courage to go through every obstacles in life is her greatest challenge'.

Shivamogga

-Bhanu Prashath

A place to be Shivamogga is a beautiful district in the state Karnataka. I grew up in this place and have a lot of memories attached to it. My dad being in the bank made us travel a lot to different places, but my love for my home town remains the same. The summer vacations spent in the grandma's place is still relishing. It is the abode of nature and abundance of culture.

I am very glad to have got such a nice opportunity to share about my home town. Shivamogga the city (district headquarters) lies on the bank of the river Tungabhadra. It is popularly known as 'Gateway of Malnad'. Malnad region in Karnataka is the abode of mountains, lush green lands, mother of several waterfalls. It has green paddy leaves, areca nut, and coconut groves.

It is also home to several great dynasties and kingdoms. It is a place of enchanted beauty. It is one of the important centers of learning. There are many popular schools and colleges that students throng to get admission.

There are many places of culture and heritage. Some places are Keladi, Ikkeri, and Koodali. These are the places that depict the rich culture of Karnataka. This is also a historical place and has a lot of religious significance.

Some of the other places to visit are: Dabbe falls, Kodachadri hills, Agumbe Ghats, Mandagadde Bird Sanctuary, and of course the world famous jog falls. The beautiful nature has helped several great poets and writers. I must confess it is in this place I realized I have a zeal for literature.

Some eminent Kannada writers like Kuvempu, UR Ananthamurthy (jnanapeetha awardees) and G.S Shivarudrappa (Popularly known as Rastrakavi) all belong to Shimoga. The cuisine is mouth-watering I must say. Tambali, Sasive, Majjigehuli, Holige, Todadevu will make sure to challenge our diet and appetite. After having said this, Shivamogga is a wonderful place to be. Do visit Shivamogga to be blessed by Mother Nature.

Bhanu Prashanth

Bhanu Prashanth is a researcher and educator. She has a great passion for reading and writing. To nurture this passion she started her own Ignitron Literary services. Being a prolific speaker, she tries to bring in equality in all her speeches as well in her writings.

She has co-authored for several books and anthologies. For her, writing is a healing process and she aspires to become one of the inspiring writers.

Andhra Pradesh..

-Leela Oduri Relangi

AP Popularly known as the rice bowl of India.. Which is one of the 8th largest state in India...

The place which is best for tourism...
Where the people followed the traditionalism..

The state which has millions of temples..
Where tirupati is one of the best example..

The state which is most famous for festivals...
Bcs people here believe that there is a god arrival...

Ap is most beautiful place filled wth greenary.. Which has one of the best scenary.....

Hyderabad is the capital of this state...
Where people vistit to see this place from different states...

Hyderabad is famous for charminar...
To see this wth two eyes its really makes u a wonder...

Andhra is most famous for the food...
Here the people hearts are filled wth good...

Andhra is the mother land to a farmer....
So the people here treated a farmer like a leader...

Hyderabad is most famous for chicken biryani... Many people here gives u a best company....

The state where people speak different languages...
And people here stayed in different villages...

The traditional wear in ap is saree....
The time u spend here is really a best memory...

Its not enough to describe about AP in words...   Bcs for many people AP is the world always a place in their hearts...

Different languages....
Different Villages...!!

Different people..... Different attitude ..!!
Same love.... Same kindness...!!

<u>Leela Oduri Relangi</u>

Leela oduri was born in Feb 28 in Tanuku ,
Andhrapradesh and now she is 18 years old and at
present she is   studying   BTech (Computer Science
Engineering)in Sri Vasavi Engineering college,
pedatadepalli,west Godavari district.
She is the co-author for anthologies named " the Eden
of memories " , "the resilient pen" etc. and one
magazine named Tare zame par. She always writes
what she feel in her heart. She loves to read , write ,

dance and act. She is open hearted and extrovert and loves to make others laugh .She never give up on those who take care for her! You all contact her through her Insta I'd : @_a_tale _of_hearts _
The page that I post everything that I write.

Uttrakhand- The Land of Gods

-Samiksha Kukreti

The 27th state of Republic of India, Devbhoomi Uttarakhand was formed in the year 2000. It's a destination to explore the riches of Indian culture and natural beauty of nature. The people of Uttrakhand are commonly known as Pahadis and they are known for their unity, calm nature n loyalty. Here people are deep rooted in their religion. People are superstitious for any new thing they do in their lives and depend on the astrological Forecast to leave no stone unturned to do that work.

Here people are more intrigue by their tribal folk dance. Chhopati, Chounphula, Jhumeila, Basanti, Mangal Barada Nati, Bhotiya Dance, Chancheri, Chhapeli, Choliya Dance, Jagars, Jhora, Langvir Dance, Langvir Nritya, Pandav Nritya, Ramola, S, Thali-Jadda, and Jhainta are the folk dance forms. Mostly Pahadi women abrade Sarong, a mantle-type dress, tightened with a blouse and an Odani and Khorpi. Rangwali pichora abrade by married women which dipicts prosperity. In the land of gods, Besides Ganges river in the foothills of Garhwal Himalayan range, surrounded by Shivalik range.

The gateway to the chardham i.e. Rishikesh is situated. Which is four desired Holi temples. Kedarnath, Badrinath, Gangotri, and Yamunotri. Hindi and Garhwali language is widely spoken here. If you are being faced between a rock and a hard plate and Sneaking for a paradise on earth to assimilate yoga in Rishikesh, India. Rishikesh is the most tranquil place and a magnet for spiritual seekers."Yoga in Rishikesh" bid internationally certified yoga teacher training in India in an apple of pie order.

Emphasizing on the customary ancient style of Hatha - yoga., Ashtanga yoga and vinyasa yoga. Rishikesh is the genesis of yoga in India, where many yoga masters pull out all the stops and practised yoga and meditation. A stunning Adorable place, The land of Gods "Uttrakhand" has it's own natural beauty.

Samiksha kukreti

Samiksha kukreti is a millenium girl born on 1st January, 2000. She is currently pursuing engineering in biotechnology. She is Nineteen years old and hails from Haridwar (Uttrakhand) but brought up in New Delhi and Rajasthan. She is a girl of words, an avid reader and a budding creative writer and poet. writing is her first love. Besides writing, She is a trained kathak dancer. She has done Prabhakar in kathak dance from Prayag Sangeet samiti, Allahabad. She lives life according to the rthym of her own drum and extremely passionate about writing. Her debut book is "Edge Of Mellinnium". She can be contacted at 1010samiksha@gmail.com Instagram: iam_samikshakukreti

Welcome to Thiruvananthapuram

-Rubal Choudhary

Enriched by Nature and abundance of water, Kerala with a capital Thiruvananthapuram is situated on south Western coastal state of India. A small state with it's long coastline, located on the tropical Malabar coast, one of the most popular tourist distinctions in the country. It is a famous of it's tourism inventiveness and beautiful backwaters. Kerala holds a tag line which says- God's own country. Kerala is well known for it's beaches, back- waters in Kollam and Alappuzha, mountain ranges in Munnar, Ponmudi and Wayanad and National Parks and wildlife sanctuaries at Periyar, Evavikulam and many more.

The agenda is to promote ecologically comfort tourism, which focuses on the local culture, wilderness experience, volunteering and personal growth to the local population. Attempts are taken to minimize the adverse effects of traditional tourism on the natural environment honor of local people, enhance the cultural. Kerala's culture is mainly of Hindu in origin.

Kerala has a rich cultural heritage. It's diverse culture is influenced by Hinduism, Christianity and Islam. The traditions of Kathakali and Mohiniattam are highly developed art forms that have developed from their folk origins into highly evolved classical dance forms.

Kathakali is a 300 year old dance form developed simply in Kerala and combining the performing art forms of ballet, opera, pantomine and masque.Elegant scriptures, music and dance forms can be seen in the historic development of Kerala's cultural traditions. OtherOther dance forms of Kerala are Kathakali, Natakom, Thiruvathirakali, Krishnanattom, Panchavadyam, Oppama and many more music forms have evolved throughout Kerala.

Onam is a time for sports and festivities and in Kerala where 1/3rd of the area is compact, covered with Canals, lakes and backwaters. The people take to their boats and country crafts to celebrate. Kerela is noted for it's variety of pancakes and steamed rice cakes from pounded rice. Kerala is the spice garden of the world. Earlier, trades from far throw lands reached Kerala in search of the spices. Enriched by Natural and abundance of water, Kerala can be reckoned as the lands of rains. It's lifelines are the two rainy seasons of Thulavarsham and Idavappathi.

Gujarat

-Rubal Choudhary

Gujarat- Jewel of Western India It is the 6th largest state in India, which is located in the Western part of India with a coastline of 1600km. Its capital is Porbandar with Ahmedabad as its Central Location. It offers a charming Beauty from Great Rann of Kutch to the hills of Saputra. Gujarat is known for its flourishment in cultural diversity. It forms an integral part of Indian Culture therefore it is known as the vibrant state. Its culture is a blend of traditions, beliefs, arts, modernization and customs. It is amongst the most industrialized state in India.

It has a lively mixture of Hinduism, Islamism, Jainism and Buddhism. History- Gujarat is also known as "Jewel of Western India". It is the main centre of the Indus valley civilization and Harappan Civilization. Gujarat has its own fairs and festivals which are very popular. They have their own wedding tradition i.e. the marriage is performed according to Vedas which consists of many prayers and vows recited in Sanskrit language. Language- People residing in Gujarat are commonly known as Gujaratis and the main language spoken by them is Gujarati.

Whereas people of Kutch speaks Kutchi. Costumes- They have their special culture of dressing. The women wears Chaniyo and Choli, while men wears Chorno and Kediyu. The jewelry worn by them are made up of silver. The outfits usually have thread work, use of beads and small patches. Cuisines- It is known for one of the healthiest cuisines in India and are usually vegetarian.

The most famous dishes are Chiwada, pathra, dhokla, khaman while sweet dishes are dhoodh pak, jalebi and mohanthal. Music and dance- It's folk music is called as Sugam Sangeet, while the instrument used are- turi, jautar, bungal and pava. The folk dance raas Garba is very popular of Gujarat when Chaniya- choli is worn by women and Kediyu by men and they dance during Navratri celebration.

Rubal Choudhary

Rubal Choudhary from Gurgaon, Haryana. She is 19 years and currently pursuing English Hons. from Delhi University. She loves to research and write articles of different Genres. She is good in making sketches and paintings and wants to aspire to become IAS. She believes write until it suits as Natural as to respire.

Andhra Pradesh and Food

-Rahul Pasumarthy

Every state has its own culture, resources, geographical conditions and parks, beaches, temples and all. Every place In India is a must visit place in meanwhile, if you're listing places to visit you must add Andhra Pradesh in it If you are foodie then you can't avoid this once you visit it. It is also called as Rice bowl of india. It is famous for spicy foods and as well sweets. Red chilli is produced abundance in this state, which added so much flavour to the foods.

Ragi is the food which is most commonly used in rayalaseema regin and uttarandhra is famed for jaggery and it also has a vast costal area and also well known for sea foods. Red chilli and gongura leaves are peculiar in Andhrapradesh, these are widely used in preparing pickles, chutneys and curries.
Following are the dishes we must taste atleast once in our lifetime.

1. Pulihora. Also called a chitranam and tamrind rice it give sour and salty taste at the same time. Tamrind, curry leaves,peanuts, are the main ingredients. It finds

its place in the kitchen during festivals and auspicious occasions.

2. Avakaya pachadi (andhra style mango pickle) It is made up of sour mango's and spices. Andhra is famous for diffrest types of mangos pickles. Even we can also add garlic, masturd seeds for taste. In pickles avakaya can get 10 out of 10.

3. Hyderabad chicken biryani. This state has given the new definition for it. Which flavours know for worldwide for its taste and smell. It made up of long grain rice, spiced and chicken pieces. Firstly it is prepared in mugals and nawabs kitchen's. Some other biriyani like fish,mutton, egg and vegetable biriyani is aslo famous

4. Gutti vankaya curry. It is the famous curry in every house. It cooked with stuffed eggplants(black brinjals). Deep fried vegitables and powder of spices is stuffed in the brinjals and cooked. It mostly served with steam rice.

 5.panasa pattu koora (andhra jack fruit curry) It made with jackfruit and cooked with fiery masalas and decorated with cashew for taste

6.boorelu(deep fried sweet dumplings) A regular hit during all Telugu festivals, boorelu is joyously prepared and enjoyed in all Telugu households. Rice flour dumplings are stuffed with aromatic coconut and chana dal mixture.

Apart from this many foods like andhra lamb curry, punugulu, green gram dosa, andhra gongura panchadi, crispy andhra bhindi, ragi ball ,curry leaf powder. Andhra is famous for spicy foods, sea foods. Most for the recipes are from mughals, kings, nawabs kitchen. They all follow the old techniques and methods.

<u>Rahul pasumarthy</u>

Rahul pasumarthy is 20 years old, a boy from vizianagaram. he is a CA student apart from his studies, he writes stories and motivational quotes, he is a moody writer and bookaholic. his dream is to inspire millions of people in following their dreams and motivate them to face their failure and believe and fall in love, he writes about life, love, pain, healing and recovery.He is an artist by mood, & a writer by passion.

My Village is My World

-Deepya Chakinarapu

My Village is My World "Hey... See those green paddy crops... Wow amazing right. I have never seen them before." "Excuse me sir, what is the name of this village?"asked Rishi to the villager. "This is Kaleshwaram. Atleast do you know that you are in a village which is in Telangana state? " questioned the villager. " yeah I know that. I came to see your village.

Its so beautiful"replied Rishi and started walking into the village. Rishi started gazing at a lady who is carrying three pots one over the other on her head without any fear of spillage of water from those well crafted, clay made, beautifully decorated pots.Rishi captured the image of the sweat drop which is rolling down her cheek. "Hey why are you taking my photo?How dare you?"screamed the lady at Rishi."Hey I am new to this village. I came for a trip.

I didn't capture you but the pots which I have never seen" said Rishi and somehow escaped from her. "Hey grandpa.. Will you show me your village in your bullock cart" asked Rishi to an old man who is passing by. " Iam going to my farm. If you want to see that then you can come betaa" said the old man. Rishi jumped into the bullock cart and sat on the dried grass which acted as a cushion in the cart. The old man whipped the bullocks to increase the speed.

The mud road started roaring because of the iron casing around the wooden wheel and is emitting dusty mud which made Rishi to cough for a while. "grand pa why didn't you wear a shirt,it's so hot right" asked Rishi."A towel on my shoulder is enough for me and I am comfortable with this betaa" said the old man. Rishi took the photographs of the huts which are on either sides of mud road. " Grandpa I have a question. Why the house roofs are made up of leaves and why not concrete"asked Rishi.The oldman smiled and said"we only know how to earn for our food. Beyond that we can't betaa".

"hey look at that river. Wow... amazing.. Grandpa what is the name of this river? " asked Rishi. " It is Godavari river. Do you know the importance of this place?" asked the old man. "please tell me naa" pleaded Rishi. "Three rivers the Godavari, the pranahitha and the saraswati join together and form a sangam called Thriveni sangam. People from all parts of the world come to visit this place. This place is also known as

Southern Kashi."said the old man. "Grandpa.. What are they doing? "asked Rishi by pointing his hand to some people who are on the banks of river holding huge nets. " ha ha they are fishing.

Fish and prawns are so tasty here.You can never find such kind of fish anywhere in this world." "Stop it grandpa....my mouth is watering". "Betaa did you visit the temple?"asked old man." " Hoo I won't visit temples. They are just boring" said Rishi. " No you should visit once because this temple has a speciality. Lord Shiva and Lord Yama idols are placed on a single stone and worshipped together which is possible only here and one more interesting fact is that the milk and water which are used for the abhisheka of these idols gets directly mixed with the river godavari through a channel which is connected to this temple and river"said the oldman. "wow.. quite interesting.

Then I will visit it"."Betaa we reached our farm,get down".Rishi could see only small leaves grown in rows.He was surprised to see and couldn't stop his curiosity. "Grand pa what are these leaves?These plants have no stem at all. What these leaves will give you?" asked Rishi. "These leaves will give us tobacco which is used in manufacturing cigarettes".Rishi went close to those plants and felt the smell of them.His eyes suddenly encountered tall trees which are forming a fence around the farm and are swinging rhythmically due to wind .

" Grand pa what are those trees?"asked Rishi." Do you know white wine? " " I know red wine but what is this white wine"? The old man went near the tree, removed the dried leaves which were spread on the ground and took a pot out of it. He went to Rishi and said " open your mouth."Rishi did what he said.Old man lifted the pot, white wine gushed from the conical neck and reached the throat of Rishi.

"Wow what a taste! sweet, sour and intoxicating. I liked it" said Rishi in a drowsy tone. Grand pa took him to his hut and made him to sleep on a cot woven with coir. Rishi woke up around 11PM and started questioning by staring at the sky, with twinkling stars and moon............. Why these things are not in the city where I live? How these people are living happily with what they have? How these people are maintaining peace in their lives? Why am I not born here?

Hindu Fest

-Deepya Chakinarapu

"Mom... Iam so hungry. Put something to eat" said Krish, a seven year old kid, after a tiresome match by throwing his cricket bat on sofa.Mom went into the kitchen and shouted "Krish wash your face and come soon". Krish was eagerly waiting for the food on dining table. Soon mom brought something in a bowl and gave to Krish. "Mom what is this?" asked Krish. "That is UGADI PACHHADI dear" replied mom. Krish took two sips of that pachhadi and said "Mom it's so tasty. So sweet but at the same time sour, mixed with bitterness and salty.Mom! Is this festival celebrated only in Telangana?" asked Krish. " No dear.. It is also celebrated in Karnataka, AndhraPradesh,Maharashtra and also in Manipur." said mom.

" Mom! some of my friends are wishing me new year. Is today new year? "asked Krish. " Yes Krish... Ugadi is celebrated every year on the first day of the Chaitra month in the Hindu luni-solar calendar. This day is considered very auspicious and is considered as New year also." "Mom.. can you bring me some more chutney? " asked Krish by licking his fingers. She went into kitchen and brought some more."

"Mom I liked this raw mango very much. Its so tempting". " Krish! do you know that each ingredient in this chutney has its own importance." "Oo! really.. What is that maa?" "Jaggery for happiness, pepper for anger, tamarind for disgust,neem for sadness, mangoes for surprise,salt for fear. These are the six basic emotions that every human has. Combination of these emotions balances our life Krish and you should celebrate every moment of your life like new year with 1great enthusiasm. "Yeah... Sure maa. I think preparing this dish is so simple. Please teach me naa. I will prepare this dish for next ugadi" asked Krish. " All you need is just six ingredients which I told earlier. Firstly soak tamarind in water , in the mean while cut raw mangoes into pieces, collect neem flowers, grind the pepper, put jaggery in some water untill it melts. Extract tamarind pulp after ten minutes and mix all the ingredients. Now add little salt to it.That's it.

The proportions of these ingredients are your wish which denotes that, it's you who brings more happiness or more sadness into your life. YOU ARE THE CREATOR OF YOUR OWN LIFE..... KRISH." " yeah...

sure maa... Get ready to next ugadi to eat my recipe"
said Krish with an innocent smile.

A

Deepya Chakinarapu

She is Sai Deepya Chakinarapu an Indian author, graduate in civil engineering from NIT warangal, founder at Uncertified Writings, an online writing platform. Officer at Indian Oil Corporation Ltd and marketer at Pro Healthywayz International. She is an expert in writing fiction with non fictitious emotion. Her upcoming Novels are A Lusty Death, The Unsaid Love (part 1)You can contact her through following links -

Facebook:https://www.facebook.com/uncertifiedwritings/

Instagram:https://www.instagram.com/uncertifiedwritings/

Twitter   :https://twitter.com/DChakinarapu?s=08

Meghalya

-Pankhi Sharma

Indian States And Traditions As a secular country we are diverse with many things, from the time we are born and are taught according to our customs, religion, language, status. We naturally adopt to our surroundings. India is such a nation to be filled with diversity which is worth seeing. Starting from top, we are welcomed with eastern traditions of himalayas, himachal pradesh and moving to north eastern region of Darjeeling, Assam, Meghalaya.

These north eastern states are blessed with various cultures and traditions holding a community together for years. People with different languages celebrate various festivals according to their own customs. I being from Assam can tell you that within the state we are filled with hundreds of communities, but the commonest one is bihu, our main festival. Bihu is related to cultivating. The happiness of successful cultivations are shown through merrymaking like dance, organising uruka(food fiesta), prayers to fire god, playing some local games, cultural nights.

As a farmer's state we are blessed with loads of own cultivation. And almost all our ancestors do had a field and still we have them as a treasure. The bihu being celebrated thrice a year comes with three phases of cultivation. First comes the Rongali bihu which marks the new year with crops full of field ready to be cultivated, starts in the month of April on the onset of monsoon season. The second phase comes in November called Kati Bihu which means no crop days.

Prayers are offered to tulsi plant by planting one in front of the house and lighting earthen diyas in fields to protect the crops. And the last one comes in the month of January as Bhogali Bihu, when the crops are ready and ready to be eaten and sell off in market. But the common thing we do all throughout this festival is wearing our traditional attire and dancing do the beats of dhol, pepa and gogona.

The tradi wears goes with the women wearing muga paat mekhela chadar and the boy with dhoti and the shirt made of paat muga. Every people are here seen with these clothes dancing in tune to the bihu songs. The most important part is the food fiesta being organised in every household. You see, we the peoples of Assam are foodies and lovers of spices. Without some strong homemade spices and chillies our menu is incomplete.

Having the boiled rice with cream curd or milk and adding some jaggery to that,cheera, akhoi or muri with the dairy products with some pithas and ladus is the perfect jolpan or the early breakfast for us. And the lunch goes with rice, mati mahor dal (black dal), masor tenga(sour fish curry), duck curry,chicken curry with laai saag, aloo pitika (smashed potato), khaar, mutton curry, maas pura (smoked fish), dal chutney, rkheer,curd.

 Lot more can be added, according to different customs but that's the standard thali I mentioned. Served in the bell metal dishes, glass and bowl as a platter is mouth watering, that can't be denied.

The customs of any state can go beyond and it really can't be fitted in a page. Though wrapping up here, I hope by reading these some of you might get the idea of coming to Assam and get a taste of us.

Bio

<u>Pankhi Sarma</u>

This is Pankhi Sarma the compiler of very first own anthology THE UNSPOKEN TALES OF A HERO anthology. She is 21 year old girl currently a final year B.tech student from GIMT Guwahati Assam. She is also the founder of SOUL EXPLORERS and WRITERS JUGALABANDI groups of instagram. She is also a published co- author of many anthologies and a compiler for two antholgies. Though an engineer by professsion, but writing comes first with the starting of the day. Winner at many writing contests and has some articles published in local magazines.She is a bundle of joy to her parents and laids her interests mostly in reading and writing. Her inspiration to write is AUTHOR CHETAN BHAGAT and her favourite writer is AUTHOR NOVONEEL CHAKRABORTY. Writing is not only a passion but a solace to her life where she finds the answers to her messy world. She is a literature lover, a social worker to her joint NGO " naba bhaskar foundation" and has been to various open mic sessions. Being a scribbler and a bibliophile, she loves clicking photographs and also a part time blogger and a content writer. An active organiser of events too. She loves painting and crafting as well. A dreamer to world and a explorer to her life. You can reach her on instagrasm @pankhi_sarma or mail her at pankhurisarma123@gmail.com

The Mirchi City

- Tejaswi Vajinepalli

Hello Readers, I am Tejaswi from Guntur and would like to tell about my place 'Guntur' which is also called the "Mirchi city" and the reason is that we are the largest exporters of Mirchi. Another famous thing that we export is cotton. People over here are devotional so we have lot of temples in the area. The food you get here is the most important attraction to anyone who comes over here and that is the same reason why people from Guntur find it difficult to adjust elsewhere especially with regard to food.

There are different kinds of food that are avail_able that you make your taste buds on your tongue go craving and wanting more. I would like to tell you more about the food as I am a foodie. Menu is more or less the same menu of the South Indian cuisine but the taste differs from one state to another state. In Tamilnadu, Pongal is more famous. In Telangana, Biryani is famous.

In Karnataka, Udupi Sambar is famous. In Andhra Pradesh, every item in the menu is famous. You get spicy and tasty food here with all the ingredients added heavily in every item to savor your taste buds. However, the main attraction lies in the evening snack items, Bajji, Punugulu and Masalas are the extremely mouthwatering food items in Guntur. Though these are available elsewhere as well but the nativity is the underlying foundation for taste especially for these items. Cost of living is pretty economical if you want to rent out a house and live, if you are buying one, it would be difficult.

Land is extremely expensive due to the new capital that has been announced in the neighboring town. Guntur is a district in which there is Guntur town. I am specifically mentioning about the Guntur town in Guntur District of Andhra Pradesh. And last but not least is the pickles of Andhra.

Andhra Pickles has a wide market in International outlets as well because of the nativity and spice of course the taste. Whenever you find a Telugu person living else where he will obviously have a jar of pickle and some home cooked snack items that are Andhra specials as well in jars with him. Though there are many attractions in Guntur but what I love about my place is food.

Tejaswi Vajinepalli

Tejaswi Vajinepalli is an avid reader and a passionate writer. He loves to Express himself through his words. He is currently employed in IT Industry and based out of Chennai.

A Sweet & Sour Trip to the Kitchen of Traditional Bengali Cuisine

-Suchismita Ghoshal

Bengali food has always been a centre of attraction when it comes to a mouthwatering discussions of food. Bengali food that originated & evolved in the region of Bengal ,situated in the eastern subcontinent of India is rich & has a gratifyingly wide range of heart melting foods from snacks to main course to sweets. The basic course generally remains the same with rice & fish playing a dominant role, probably this is the reason why bengalis are mentioned as " Maachhe-Bhaate-Bangali" where "Maachh" is fish & "Bhaat" means boiled rice in Bengali language.

 A bengali meal/lunch follows a multi-course tradition where the food is served course-wise usually in a specific format, labelling it as the only meal of our subcontinent to have a different style & its own convention. Generally a bengali lunch starts with a "Shukto" (a bitter preparation), followed by "Shak" (a leafy vegetables preparation), Daal (pulses), variety of vegetable curries, then main course with fish/mutton/chicken/egg curry, chutney (sweet-sour saucy item) & ends with sweet dish like curd & other traditional sweets like "Sandesh" & "Rosogolla".

Such an outstanding range of foods served accordingly as a row! Just like this, a bengali dinner too goes stunning with something " Kosha" (stuffed gravy of veg or non veg item) or "Kalia" (spicy gravy of food items) along with boiled rice & salads. Bengal, with rich cultivating land, has a great history of producing varied & a good quality rice. As presaid, Bengal has a really head-turning fish culture, it fetches some delicious fishes like ruhi, katla, pabda, tangra, koi, hilsa, pomfret, vetki, chitol, bata & other sea animals like prawns & crabs.

Variety of dairy products like ghee, butter, curd & a huge variety of cheese made sweet dishes. Mustard oil is mostly used in preparing different cuisines along with soya oil sometimes. The foodie bengalis are not a half inch lazy to make their breakfast a little less delicious; from "Luchi- Tarkari" (a flour made round shaped food items like kachoris) to "Muri"(rice in puffed form) , "Chira"(beaten form of rice) , "Khoi" (fried form of rice) , some fruits & milk etc have traditionally enriched the plates of bengalis' breakfast tables for decades.

A variety of spices and their mixes are used in preparing Bengali cuisines, the common ones being halud(turmeric), jira(cumin), dhone(coriander), radhuni, kaloo jeera(black onion seeds), dried chilli powder, posto(poppy seeds), methi(fenugreek), mouri(fennel), peyaj(onion), ada(ginger), narikel(ripe coconut), and a combination of five spices called "Panch phoron" comprises of kalo jeera, cumin, black mustard seeds, fenugreek & fennel. Bengalis, especially make their lazy weekends more special with spicy non-veg cuisines of "Jhal" (spicy food items) , "Jhol" (gravy) , "Korma", "Kopta", "Kalia" etc.

Some non-veg food delicacies are "Kochi Pathar Jhol" , "Chingri Malaikari", " Ilish bhapa" etc which can easily make anyone crave for random visits in Bengal. Some popular snacks like "Jhal Muri" (muri mixed with chopped onion, boiled potato, tomato, cucumber, diff. spices & other ingredients), "Chira Bhaja", "Singara" (samosa) & again some influential delicious food items for years old dynasties of Mughals & British in Bengal are Chili Chicken, Kababs, Chowmin, Biriyani etc have been warmly owned by bengalis for years. Lists of bengali foods are even more long. Though I have tried to at least peep through every nook & corner of bengalis' kitchen, I feel I still have much left to say keeping my taste buds in control now. Last but not the least, We, bengalis welcome our guests as Gods in our homes & never forget to satisfy their fantasies over food.

<u>Suchismita Ghoshal</u>

Hailing from a small city Malda, West Bengal, Suchismita dreams high to touch the sky. She is an avid reader, writer, poet, muser, scribbler, storyteller, published author, blogger, nature lover, social worker & a freelance model. She will soon complete her graduation on Zoology. Her debut book titled "Fields of Sonnet" will soon be launched. She aspires to become a great author & book reviewer in future.

A note from the Author

64

Dear Citizens,

This is our mother land . Let's take an oath and love it
and never disrespect our nation. We as a whole may
bring honour to the nation.
Let's start respecting the diversities, and give equal
importance to each on of it , we must avoid the usage of
taboo words.

Live and let live.

Jai Hind

65

You can contact the Publisher at:

www.fanatixx.in